Ugly Duckling

Louis Weber, C.E.O.
Publications International, Ltd.
7373 North Cicero Avenue
Lincolnwood, Illinois 60646

Manufactured in China.

8 7 6 5 4 3 2 1

ISBN: 0-7853-2609-X

Publications International, Ltd.

Ugly Duckling

Cover illustrated by
Deborah Colvin Borgo

Illustrated by
Susan Spellman

Adapted by
Sarah Toast

Publications International, Ltd.

*I*t was a beautiful summer morning in the country. Beside a pond, a mother duck was sitting on her nest. She had been sitting a long time, waiting for her eggs to hatch.

Finally the eggs began to crack. "Peep, peep," said the newly hatched ducklings.

"Quack, quack," said their mother. "You are the sweetest little yellow ducklings I have ever seen! Are you all hatched?" But the biggest egg hadn't hatched yet.

The tired mother duck sat down again on the last egg and waited. When the egg finally cracked, out tumbled a clumsy gray duckling. He was bigger than the others and very ugly.

"Peep, peep," said the gray baby. The mother duck looked at him.

"He's awfully big for his age," she said. "And he looks different than all my other ducklings. I wonder if he can swim."

The next day the sun shone brightly. The mother duck led all of her ducklings down to the pond.

"Quack, quack," she told them.

One after the other, the eager ducklings hopped into the blue water. They bobbed and floated like little corks. They already knew how to paddle their legs and swim! All of the new ducklings swam very nicely, even the ugly one.

The mother duck was very pleased. She decided to take her ducklings to the farmyard to meet the other ducks.

"Quack, quack," she said. "Follow me! Keep your legs far apart and waddle this way. Then bow your heads and say 'quack.'"

The little ducklings did as their mother did. But the other ducks in the barnyard gathered around them and said, "Look at how ugly the gray one is!" One of them even tried to bite the ugly duckling on the neck.

"Leave him alone!" cried the mother duck. But the poor duckling was chased around the barnyard and mistreated by everyone, even his own brothers and sisters.

How sad the ugly little duckling was!
Every day the hens and the other ducks
pushed him and made fun of him.

At last the ugly duckling had enough
and ran away. He finally came to a swamp
where the wild geese lived. The tired little
duckling stayed all night in the swamp.

In the morning, the wild geese found
him. "You don't look like we do," the geese
said to him, "but that's all right. You can stay
here with us for now." Just then a hunter's
dog walked by, and the geese flew off in
alarm. The scared duckling stayed as still
as he could for a very long time.

When he was sure that the dog was gone, the little duckling set off across the meadows. It was dark when he came to a crooked little hut. The door was open just a crack, and in went the little duckling.

An old woman lived in the hut with her cat and her hen. She felt sorry for the ugly little duckling and let him stay.

The little duckling couldn't purr or lay eggs, so the cat and the hen picked on him day and night. This made the duckling miss the pond and bobbing up and down in the water, so he finally left the crooked little hut.

The duckling found a lake where he could dive to the bottom and pop back up again to float in the water. The wild ducks ignored him because he was so ugly.

Autumn came, and with it clouds and cold winds. One evening just at sunset, a flock of beautiful, big birds with powerful wings flew overhead. Their feathers were shining white, and they had long, graceful necks.

The sight of these swans, for that is what they were, made the ugly duckling wish that he could be so beautiful. The ugly duckling felt a strong bond with the swans and was sad to see them flying away.

The weather got colder and colder. It got so cold that one morning the duckling was stuck in the ice on the lake. It was fortunate for him that a passing farmer freed him from the ice.

The farmer put the duckling under his arm and carried him home. The farmer's naughty children were excited and wanted to play with the duckling. The duckling thought they were going to hurt him, and in his fright he ran right into a milk pail. Then he flapped into a bowl of butter and flopped into a barrel of flour. He made quite a mess!

The farmer's wife chased the ugly duckling right out of the house.

The children ran after the ugly duckling, trying to catch him. The duckling found a hiding place under some bushes. As the snow fell around him, he lay still until the children went indoors.

The ugly duckling had a very bad winter. Food was hard to find, and the frosty winds howled. But when spring finally arrived with the warm sun shining and the robins' song in the air, the ugly duckling had survived.

Filled with the joy and happiness of spring, the duckling spread his wings to fly. My, how strong and powerful his wings had become over the long, hard winter!

The duckling flew over green gardens and orchards. Then he saw three swans floating on a lake, and he felt a certain bond with them.

The ugly duckling wanted to be near the beautiful swans, even if they might be cruel. He landed on the water and swam toward them. When the three swans saw the duckling, they went to meet him.

As they drew near, the ugly duckling bowed his head to the water, expecting to be treated badly. Upon looking down, he saw that there was another beautiful swan, a fourth swan floating in the lake.

It was his own reflection. He was no longer a clumsy, ugly bird. He was a swan!

His ugly gray feathers had dropped away as he grew over the long winter, and now he had shiny, white feathers, big, powerful wings, and a long, graceful neck!

"I look like you," he said excitedly to the other swans. "I am beautiful!"

When he looked at the three swans, the bond he felt was even stronger than before. They seemed to know how difficult it was to be an ugly duckling, and they also seemed to share his newfound joy.

The other swans made a circle around him and stroked him with their beaks. All that the young swan had gone through made him truly appreciate his newfound happiness, and he saw the beauty of everything that surrounded him.

He ruffled his feathers and thought aloud, "I never dreamed of such happiness when I was an ugly duckling."

The
End